BIG BLUE

Shelley Gill • illustrated by Ann Barrow

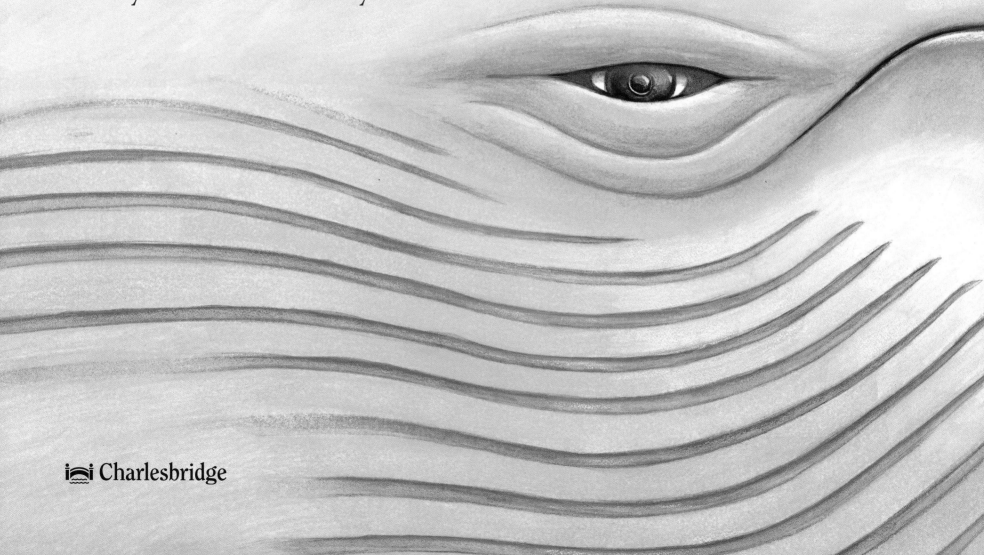

ini Charlesbridge

Every night before I go to sleep, I make a wish. Someday I want to swim with a blue whale. And every night I dream of whales. In the darkness, as I swim lazily toward sleep, tiny lights appear. They skim and swirl, violet, crimson, and gold, like stars blinking, like tiny fish twinkling in an ocean of night. I imagine myself twirling through space, deep-water space.

Then, only shadows at first, they appear. My dreams are filled with huge gliding shapes, swirling in turquoise waters. Whales—blue whales.

I tell my mother my wish. She doesn't laugh.

"Dreams come true every day," she says.

But how? How could I swim with a blue whale?

I know just about everything a kid can know about whales. I know that whales are mammals, not fish; they breathe air. The newborn calf, at 25 feet, will be the fastest-growing creature on earth. The mother must produce 160 gallons of milk a day to feed a baby that gains 10 pounds an hour—250 pounds a day—a rate of growth nearly fast enough to be seen! Being big is important because bigger is warmer in the cold oceans.

A blue whale's heart is the size of a car, weighing two tons and pumping 60 gallons of blood with each beat. The heart valves look like Frisbees, and the aorta is big enough for a small black bear to crawl through.

At 20 knots per hour, blue whales are the fastest swimmers in the sea. Their yearly migrations cover thousands of miles. The biggest dinosaur ever found probably weighed just over 80 tons—the biggest blue whale weighed more than twice that. She was 168 feet long and weighed about 160 tons. She was killed in 1928 by Yankee whalers in Antarctica.

Before people began hunting them, blue whales knew no fear. Then humans declared war on whales. In the days before people drilled oil from the ground, lamps burned whale-oil fuel. In the old days a big whale was worth big bucks for the money its oil would bring. Men hunted whales for their baleen, blubber, and bone. Hundreds of ships full of hunters stalked whales from the top of the world to the bottom.

Long ago the seas were silent except for animals. Before big boats and the buzz of undersea cables, blue whales sang to each other from around the world. But whale songs are hardly ever heard now, except by scientists and sailors. Imagine the loudest sound you have ever heard an animal make, then multiply it a zillion times. Male blue whales make the loudest sound of any living creature—a low, moaning song that is too far down the scale for humans to hear. It's probably used to see the ocean floor through echolocation— bouncing sound waves from the bottom of the sea.

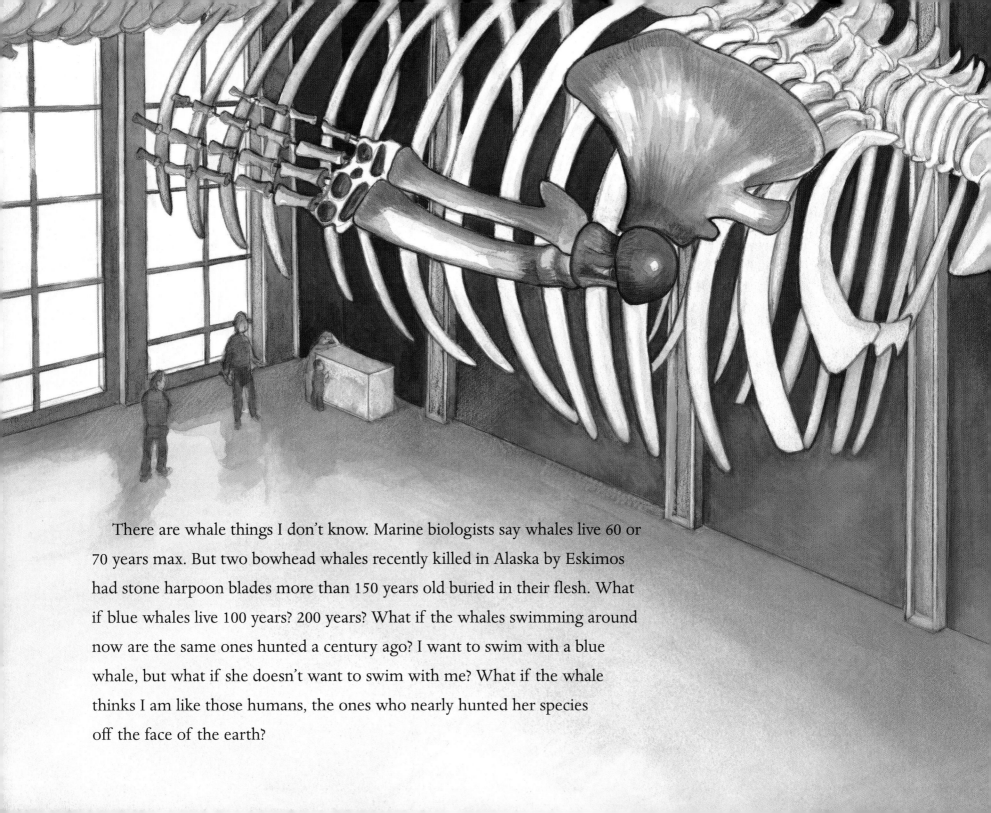

There are whale things I don't know. Marine biologists say whales live 60 or
70 years max. But two bowhead whales recently killed in Alaska by Eskimos
had stone harpoon blades more than 150 years old buried in their flesh. What
if blue whales live 100 years? 200 years? What if the whales swimming around
now are the same ones hunted a century ago? I want to swim with a blue
whale, but what if she doesn't want to swim with me? What if the whale
thinks I am like those humans, the ones who nearly hunted her species
off the face of the earth?

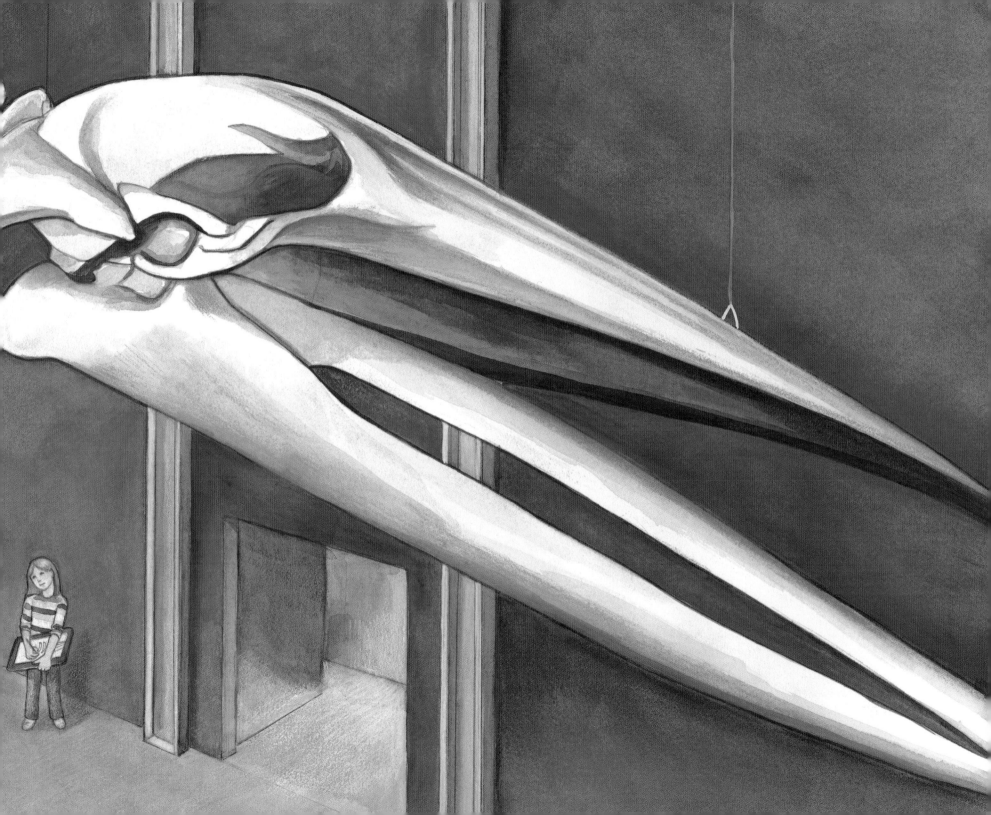

"There are no guarantees, Kye," Mom says, grinning. "We'll go where blue whales might be, and we'll go swimming. The rest is up to them."

"No way!" I shout. "You're the awesomest mom in the world!"

During the next week she calls around, and our journey begins to take shape. My mom's a writer, and she drives a whale-research boat in Alaska. She hangs out with marine biologists.

Three biologists and their kids, including my friends Lars and Steffy,
are heading to Baja, Mexico, to do research, and we can tag along.
They will be taking shots of whale tails so they can track whale migration.
Each whale tail is unique, like a fingerprint, and the marine biologists hope
to use their photographs and videos to identify the same whales off
the coast of northern California next summer.

Early each morning we roll out of our hammocks. Before Mom's coffee is ready, Lars and I use binoculars to scan the bay for whales. After breakfast the scientists take off in their panga. Lars, Steffy, and I snorkle off the rocky coast, teasing eels and small fish. In the afternoon we swim offshore and float on soft swells. We see skates and dolphins and sea lions. But no whales.

One morning El Oesta, the west wind, begins to whisper through the canyons. If El Oesta blows hard, the water will be too rough for swimming, maybe for days. My mother smiles to encourage me as I shiver into my wet suit.

Mom, Lars, and I swim away from the coral-colored cliffs, diving like dolphins in the cool Pacific water. I am resting, rocking in the sea, when Lars yells. I turn in time to see her roll, water sliding from her back like a sheet of molten silver. She is a perfect whale, deep-water blue, cold-water blue, blue scooped from mountaintops a mile beneath the sea. Big Blue.

We tread water and wait for the whale to decide. If she doesn't want to swim with me, she'll disappear.

Then Big Blue breaches, all 70 tons of her rocketing from the water, then crashing down. The sound explodes, bouncing off the sandstone cliffs.

My stomach somersaulting, I listen to the echo that lingers.

Even though I'm paddling slowly, my heart is pounding. I am afraid.

But Big Blue's not afraid. She's playing.

She rolls. Again. Then again. Big Blue rolls three times before we see her tiny dorsal fin, then she flukes. Her stocky tail looks like a giant licorice gumdrop disappearing into the sea. Has she seen us? Will she swim away? As I lose sight of her in the swell, my heart sinks.

Then Big Blue is there, swimming nearby on the surface. I suck in air
and dive, deep into the blue silence, into her world of cold and shadow.
And I am in my dream.

Little dots of light turn into shimmery squid. Red ribbons are really krill,
the tiny shrimp Big Blue eats, thousands at a time. Moon jellies pulsate like
heartbeats through thin shafts of light.

I surface in Big Blue's shadow. Her body swallows the sun. I slowly sink again. Beside her huge, gaping mouth, one grapefruit eye stares at me, curious. She's smart enough to know I'm not krill, but I am scared. I ache for air. The surface calls me. I grab a breath, shake my fear, and dive again.

I see the yellow knobs on Big Blue's belly, her pleated throat, the gaping cave of her mouth. She lifts her pectoral fin and glides by me. I turn to swim beside her. Time stops. This moment belongs to Big Blue and me. I twirl like a manta ray in her surge, dancing in the depths of her deep, blue sea.

I swim until the tiny lights appear in my vision, crimson, violet, and gold, and my burning lungs force me up. I gulp air and dive again and again, but Big Blue is gone. Gone to an alien world beneath the surface. A place as dark and mysterious as our dreams. I hang suspended, peering into the depths, holding my breath, holding on to my dream, listening for a song I can never hear.

First paperback edition 2005
Text copyright © 2003 by Shelley Gill
Illustrations copyright © 2003 by Ann Barrow
All rights reserved, including the right of reproduction in whole or in part in any form. Charlesbridge and colophon are registered trademarks of Charlesbridge Publishing, Inc.

Published by Charlesbridge
85 Main Street
Watertown, MA 02472
(617) 926-0329
www.charlesbridge.com

Library of Congress Cataloging-in-Publication Data

Gill, Shelley.
  Big Blue / Shelley Gill ; illustrated by Ann Barrow.
    p. cm.
  Summary: A young girl's dream to swim with a blue whale may finally come true when her mother, a writer, arranges for them to accompany her friends who are marine biologists on a research trip to Mexico.
  ISBN-13: 978-1-57091-352-5; ISBN-10: 1-57091-352-8 (reinforced for library use)
  ISBN-13: 978-1-57091-667-0; ISBN-10: 1-57091-667-5 (softcover)
  [1. Blue whale—Fiction. 2. Whales—Fiction. 3. Endangered species—Fiction. 4. Baja California (Mexico)—Fiction.]
  I. Barrow, Ann, ill. II. Title.
  PZ7.G3994 Bi 2003
  [Fic]—dc21   2002010534

Printed in Korea
(hc) 10 9 8 7 6 5 4 3 2 1
(sc) 10 9 8 7 6 5 4 3
Illustrations done in watercolors and colored pencil on illustration board
Display type and text type set in Dante
Color separations by Imago
Printed and bound by Sung In Printing, South Korea

Author's Note:

When my nine-year-old daughter, Kye, came home from school and asked me if she could swim with a blue whale, I was hooked! It's illegal to pursue whales, or to harass them. And for sure those were the last things we wanted to do. So we went swimming every day, hoping that one day a whale would come. And one did!

Whales have lived in harmony on this planet for 18 million years. Imagine a young blue whale. Like you, whales love to play and sleep. They zoom along the surface of the water, using their tails as sails. They spy hop to get a look around, and if their mother is not paying enough attention, they drape themselves across her blowhole, cutting off her air until she gets the picture!

Once there were some 400,000 blue whales swimming the waters of the world. My daughter and I were approached by Big Blue off the coast of Mexico. There, in the winter of 1932, 29,000 blue whales were killed in one season. To save whales, to save ourselves, I think we must examine human nature and make a choice for peace.